VALENTINE CATS

VALENTINE CATS

by Jean Marzollo
Illustrated by Hans Wilhelm

Cartwheel
·B·O·O·K·S·®

SCHOLASTIC INC.
New York   Toronto   London   Auckland   Sydney

Library of Congress Cataloging-in-Publication Data

Marzollo, Jean.
        Valentine cats / by Jean Marzollo ; illustrated by Hans Wilhelm.
            p.   cm.— (Read with me paperbacks)
        "Cartwheel Books."
        Summary: Writer cats, artist cats, and postal cats create and deliver
Valentines.
        ISBN 0-590-47596-7
        [1. Cats — Fiction.   2. Valentine's Day — Fiction.   3. Stories in rhyme.]
    I. Wilhelm, Hans, 1945 –, ill.   II. Title.   III. Series.
    PZ8.3.M4194Val   1996
    [E] — dc20   94-47816
                                                                                 CIP
                                                                                 AC

12   11   10   9   8   9/9   0   1/0

                        Printed in the U.S.A.   24

                First Scholastic printing, January 1996

For Maggie and Elwood, cool cats
　　　　　— J.M.

Writer cats get ready,

Writer cats start a card,

Writer cats need a message,

Writer cats think hard.

Writer cats find words,

Writer cats write more,

Little kittens catching
Drafts falling to the floor.

Artist cats choose paper,

Artist cats dab glue,

Artist cats shake glitter,

Artist cats paint, too.

Artist cats make hearts,

Artist cats cut more,

Little kittens catching
Scraps falling to the floor.

Postal cats make a mailbox,

Postal cats write a sign,

Postal cats fill bags,

Postal cats look fine.

Postal cats on the march,

Postal cats at the door,

Little kittens catching
Mail falling to the floor.
MEOW!

HAPPY VALENTINE'S DAY!